x

For Anna Beattie and her daddy
(who both love Pugly)

P. B.

First published in the UK in 2016 by Nosy Crow Ltd
The Crow's Nest, 10a Lant Street
London, SE1 1QR, UK

Nosy Crow and associated logos are trademarks and/or registered
trademarks of Nosy Crow Ltd

Text copyright © Pamela Butchart, 2016
Cover and illustrations copyright © Gemma Correll, 2016

The right of Pamela Butchart and Gemma Correll to be identified
as the author and illustrator respectively of this work has been asserted
by them in accordance with the Copyright, Designs
and Patents Act 1988.

All rights reserved

1 3 5 7 9 10 8 6 4 2

A CIP catalogue record for this book will be available from the British Library.

This book is sold subject to the condition that it shall not, by way of
trade or otherwise, be lent, hired out or otherwise circulated in any
form of binding or cover other than that in which it is published. No
part of this publication may be reproduced, stored in a retrieval
system, or transmitted in any form or by any means (electronic, mechanical,
photocopying, recording or otherwise) without the prior written permission
of Nosy Crow Ltd.

Printed and bound in the UK by Clays Ltd, St. Ives Plc

Papers used by Nosy Crow are made from wood grown in
sustainable forests.

ISBN: 978 0 85763 896 0

www.nosycrow.com

Chapter 1

Clem the cat
got me ICE
SKATES for my
birthday, which
is BRILLIANT
because I love
ICE and ICE
SKATING
and wearing
my awesome
BOBBLE HAT!

When I tried the ice skates on I felt
something SLIMY between my toes.

It was a piece of old lettuce.

"Erm… I MIGHT have found them in a
bin," said Clem. "Happy birthday, Pugly."

But I didn't even CARE about the bin OR
the slimy old lettuce leaf because I had a

PUGTASTIC IDEA!

"CLEM!" I screamed.

"I'm going to enter

PETS ON ICE!

It's a big ice-skating competition and it's
coming to OUR town. I saw a flyer about it
a few days ago."

I threw myself at the FLAPPY BIN LID and went tumbling into the bin.

"WHAT are you doing?!" said Clem.

"WHAT?" I shouted. "I can't hear you! I'm in the bin!"

It was a bit dark inside the bin (and SMELLY!) but I eventually managed to find the *Pets on Ice* flyer.

 3

I leapt out of the bin to show Clem.

"STAY BACK!" she hissed. "You smell disgusting! I was going to tell you about the competition. I thought we could—"

"LOOK, Clem!" I yelled as I picked baked beans off the flyer and waved it at her. "I am SO excited because I am TOTALLY going to WIN!"

"Yes, but—" Clem started but I just ignored her and put my bobble hat and scarf on. She can sometimes be a bit rude about my PUGTASTIC IDEAS and I didn't want her to kill my dream.

"Where are you going?" said Clem.

"To the ice rink to sign up for the competition, of course!" I said. "You can be my

PROFESSIONAL TRAINER.

Let's go!"

Chapter 2

As soon as we arrived at the ice rink I realised that I was going to have some SERIOUS competition. There were LOADS of dogs on the ice.

"Clem," I said. "Do you think they're all here to practise for *Pets on Ice* too?"

Clem nodded. "The FIVE BEST ACTS will get to compete in this year's competition," she said. "You know that you can have a partner if you like?"

"A partner?" I said.

Clem started to say something else but just then everyone inside the rink GASPED! We looked up and saw a FIREBALL spinning in the air above the rink!

"RUUUUUN!" I screamed.

But Clem didn't run. Then everyone started CHEERING and CLAPPING because the fireball WASN'T a fireball... It was a Pomeranian DOG!

The Pomeranian was called ROJO and he had the most AMAZING ice-skating costume EVER because it had FAKE FLAME BITS coming out of it and when he starting spinning he looked EXACTLY like a

BALL OF FIRE.

I dragged Clem over to the side of the rink so I could talk to Rojo.

"WOW! You're FAST!" I told him.

But Rojo just ignored me and STARED at Clem.

"You are a very beautiful cat," said Rojo. "I have travelled the world and never seen a face finer than yours."

Clem completely ignored Rojo and just walked away.

"Hey, Rojo," I said. "Would you like to be my SKATING PARTNER?"

"Hmmm," said Rojo. "Tell me, pug. What is your THING?"

I had no idea what Rojo meant.

"Your THING, pug. You know. Your special THING that you can do on the ice that makes the crowd go WILD! What is your ice-skating GIFT to the world?"

"Um, well, I don't think I have a thing," I said, looking down at my paws.

"Then I am sorry, my friend, but I have worked hard all my life to be the best spinning Pomeranian the people have ever seen. I cannot be your partner if you cannot add something special to my act. *Adios*."

I didn't know what "*Adios*" meant but then Rojo left so I supposed it meant goodbye.

Then Clem appeared out of NOWHERE

and gave me such a fright I SNEEZED!

Clem is ALWAYS sneaking up on me like that. It's a cat thing.

"What did HE want? Did you ask him to be your PARTNER?" she asked, sounding annoyed.

I thought Clem was being a bit weird about the partner thing but I didn't have time to ask why because I was too busy putting my skates on.

"CLEM! I need to find out what my THING is!" I said. "Watch me from the side. I'm going to try LOADS of stuff, like

≋SPINNING≋

and LEAPING

and maybe even

THE SPLITS
and – UMPPPHFFFF!"

As SOON as I stepped on the ice I fell down.

"Um, Pugly?" said Clem, as I lay on my back. "You DO know how to ice skate, right?"

"Of COURSE I know how to SKATE!" I said. "I have watched ice skating on TV for YEARS!"

Clem narrowed her eyes at me.

"But have you ever ACTUALLY done it?" she asked.

I thought about this for a bit.

"Well, no. Not on ACTUAL ice. But I've practised in the living room in front of the TV LOADS!"

I tried to get back on my feet but I slipped and fell again.

Clem shook her head and began STRAPPING ON SOME SKATES! I was

TOTALLY AMAZED!

She started to pull me around the ice until I got used to skating by myself.

"You're actually not totally awful at this," said Clem.

Pretty soon I even managed to skate BACKWARDS too (well, until I bumped into someone, that is).

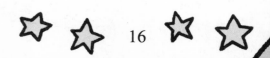

"WATCH IT!" said a voice. I turned
around to see two greyhounds in MEGA
GLAMOROUS skating costumes. I
recognised them RIGHT AWAY!

"Oh … um … sorry!" I said, and then
I hid behind Clem because just then the
music changed and the lights went down
and a HUGE spotlight shone on the middle
of the ice.

"LADIES AND GENTLEMEN …
ALL THE WAY FROM
THE USA …
IT'S THE ICE-SKATING TWINS …

JASMINE

AND GERARD!"

The crowd started cheering REALLY
LOUDLY and Jasmine and Gerard skated
round and waved and blew kisses.

Someone handed Jasmine a microphone
and the crowd went SILENT.

"Oh MY!" said Jasmine. "It's just
wonderful of you all to come and see little
old us. We couldn't be more THRILLED
to be in the UK. We LOVE the UK. Who
knows, maybe one day we'll be YOUR ice-
skating champions, too!"

19

The crowd went WILD when Jasmine said that. People began screaming and throwing flowers and some people were even crying with HAPPINESS!

Jasmine picked up some of the flowers and sniffed them.

"Why THANK you, THANK YOU! You're all as sweet as PEACH PIE!"

That's when Clem turned to me and whispered, "Pugly. We have a problem."

Clem was right. It was going to be difficult to beat Jasmine and Gerard because they were ice-skating SUPERSTARS!

Chapter 3

Once everyone EVENTUALLY stopped
cheering, the judges announced that they
had selected their TOP FIVE skaters
to compete in this year's *Pets on Ice*
competition.

I GASPED. I had NO IDEA the judges
had been watching us!

Clem STARED at the judges as they
began to announce this year's contestants.
Her eyes were SO WIDE that I think she
might have been trying to HYPNOTISE
them.

Jasmine and Gerard's names were called first.

The crowd cheered and WHOOPED as the twins skated on to the ice, holding hands.

Then the judges picked Rojo.

A sausage dog called Hugo.

And Tiny the chihuahua.

My heart sank.

"That's five, Clem," I said, glumly.

"No. It's NOT. Jasmine and Gerard are a PAIR. They count as one."

I gasped and looked back at the judges because Clem was RIGHT.

There was ONE SPOT LEFT.

Clem held my paw while we waited for the judges to announce the last act, even though Clem NEVER usually holds my paw, not even when I ask her to.

"Our final contestant will be someone

22

who has shown they are a VERY fast learner," said one of the judges.

"PUGLY!

Please join us on the ice!"

I couldn't believe it.

I WAS IN!

Chapter 4

As soon as I stepped off the ice again, Clem pulled me backstage into a dressing room. I'd never SEEN her move so fast before!

"It's very important that you look like a PROFESSIONAL ICE SKATER," she said as she whizzed around pulling out all the outfits she could find.

I had no idea why SHE was so excited about the competition but I didn't say anything because Clem is THE BEST when she's being helpful and I wanted her to find me the PERFECT ice-skating outfit.

Clem flicked through a rack of sparkly outfits until she FROZE and began purring REALLY LOUDLY.

I knew that meant she'd found something AMAZING for me to wear.

"I am NOT wearing THAT!" I yelled when Clem showed me a BRIGHT RED LEOTARD.

"You MUST!" said Clem. "It's FABULOUS."

I stared at the teeny, tiny leotard.

"Clem, it's FAR too small. It won't fit."

"Of course it will," said Clem. "Look, it's SUPER STRETCHY."

I eventually gave in and tried on the leotard and looked in the mirror.

Clem was right. It WAS fabulous!

"Now all we need is some glitter," said Clem.

I was JUST about to ask Clem what we needed glitter for when she threw an ENTIRE POT ALL OVER ME!

"Urrrrrrggggghhh! Clem, that went in my MOUTH!"

But Clem wasn't listening. She had about FIFTEEN make-up brushes in her hand and she was dusting and spreading the glitter ALL OVER my body.

"Now, LOOK!" she said as she spun me back round to face the mirror.

I hardly recognised myself.

I looked like an ice-skating

SUPERSTAR!

Chapter 5

Round One of the competition was a
GROUP SKATE. All the contestants had
to skate round the rink together while the
judges watched and gave us SCORES.

As soon as the music started, Jasmine and
Gerard LEAPT on to the ice and the crowd
cheered. They began TWIRLING and
LEAPING and GRINNING at the judges
LOADS.

Then they got ready to do their
SIGNATURE MOVE. The crowd started
whispering and pointing as Jasmine took
hold of Gerard's paws and began spinning
him around and around the ice … and
then she LET GO and he did a TRIPLE
BACKFLIP and landed on his feet. The
crowd went WILD!

Then Tiny started
SPEED SKATING

and Hugo the sausage dog did loads of
BELLY SLIDES along the ice.

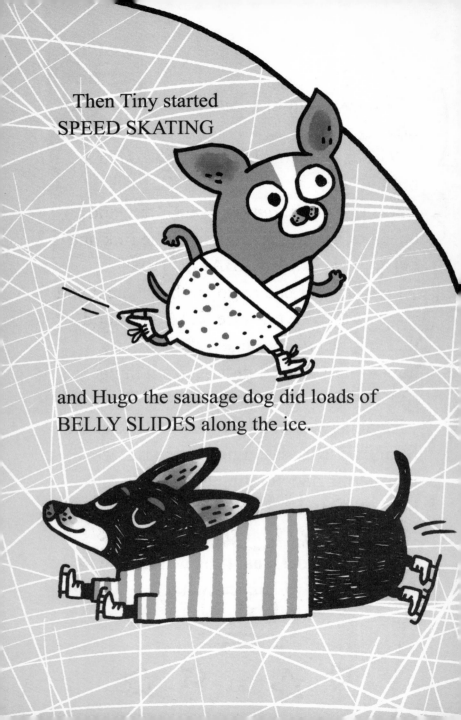

"Do you want to go on next?" Rojo asked me.

"Um… You go," I said. "I'll be on in a minute."

"Suit yourself, *amigo*," said Rojo, and he RACED into the middle of the rink and began doing his FIREBALL THING.

I knew that I had to go on the ice next and skate with everyone else, but I just stood there at the side because I didn't know how to start and I didn't have anything SPECIAL to show the judges.

I looked over at Clem who was sat in the front row. She was giving me her

WIDE EYES

which I knew meant she wanted me to

GO!

EVERYONE was showing the judges their SPECIAL MOVES. I knew I had to do SOMETHING to impress the judges, so I skated backwards as fast as I could and gave the judges a big smile as I went past them. But they didn't smile back.

"I'm never going to win, Clem," I said, skating over to the side and letting her massage my shoulders. "There's nothing SPECIAL about my act."

"You just need some INSPIRATION, Pugly," said Clem. "Think!" And she pushed me back out on to the ice.

So I did think. I closed my eyes and pictured myself as a BIRD flying across the ice.

And it WORKED! As I skated I felt myself SOARING into the air ... before I landed with a CRASH!

The judges were NOT pleased that I'd landed on the judging table.

I panicked.

I lay on my back on the table and smiled and kicked my legs in the air to make it look like the crash-landing was all part of my ACT. But the judges didn't look very pleased with me, especially when I accidentally kicked a cup of water over one of them.

I held my breath when the music stopped and the judges began announcing the scores for ROUND ONE.

"At the end of Round One, Tiny and Rojo

have each been awarded seven out of ten," said the Head Judge.

"ALRIGHT! Give me some PAW!" said Tiny as she high-fived Rojo, who puffed out his chest and winked at Clem.

"Hugo has been awarded a six, Pugly has been awarded a five and Jasmine and Gerard have scored a nine."

I got a FIVE. A FIVE! Which is halfway to a TEN! I was over the moon.

"CLEEEEEM!" I yelled as I raced over to her. "I got a FIVE!"

But Clem wasn't listening.

"Look," she said, pointing to Jasmine and Gerard, who were walking back to their dressing room.

I couldn't hear what they were saying because they were too far away, but I could see that Jasmine was SCOWLING at the judges and whispering something to Gerard.

"I saw Jasmine's face when the judges said they got nine out of ten," said Clem. "She was NOT pleased."

I was SHOCKED when Clem said that because a NINE is an EXCELLENT score and it meant that Jasmine and Gerard were actually

WINNING!

Chapter 6

Before Round Two of the competition,
all the contestants were given time
to practise and spend time with their
PROFESSIONAL TRAINERS.

"Tell me what happened out there today,"
said Clem, as she spread even MORE
glitter on me. "How ON EARTH did you
end up crashing into the judges' table?"

"Well, you said I needed inspiration," I began, nervously. "So I pictured myself as a bird…"

Clem thought about this for a minute.

"Pugly," she said. "What bird did you imagine yourself as?"

"A pigeon," I replied.

Clem closed her eyes and shook her head at me.

"SSSHHHHH!" I said, before she could tell me how stupid I was. "It's time for ROUND TWO! LOOK! The judges are coming back out!"

Clem looked REALLY EXCITED. In fact, she'd been acting a bit HYPER and WEIRD all day and I had no idea why.

In Round Two of *Pets on Ice* all of the contestants had to skate by themselves for a WHOLE ROUTINE and at the end the judges would hold up a board with a score on it.

Tiny was up first.

I was really excited about watching Tiny's routine because she can skate at

<u>SUPER FAST</u>
<u>SPEED.</u>

But Tiny DIDN'T do her routine. She whispered something to the judges and then sat down at the side with her head in her hands.

The judges all looked at each other and then one of them spoke into the microphone and said, "TINY HAS PULLED OUT OF ROUND TWO. THERFORE SHE SCORES ZERO POINTS."

The crowd GASPED and all the skaters rushed over to see if Tiny was OK.

"My ice skates," whimpered Tiny. "They're GONE!"

We all looked at Tiny's bare feet.

"Oh dear," said Jasmine. "You must have misplaced them. Perhaps you can rent some to use instead?"

Tiny looked HORRIFIED when Jasmine said that.

"They're my

she wailed. "I can't skate without my

LUCKY
SKATES!"

I felt TERRIBLE for Tiny because she was now out of the competition.

Next it was time for Rojo.

The crowd began stamping its feet and Rojo waved at everyone before pulling the hood up on his costume.

I gasped when Rojo walked past me
because he had a NEW skating costume on
and it had even more FLAME BITS and
long yellow, orange and red RIBBONS
hanging from it and I just KNEW that
when he starting spinning he was going to
look AMAZING.

Rojo skated over to where Clem was sitting and whispered something in her ear before he started. Clem rolled her eyes at him.

Rojo began skating really fast and I knew that he was preparing to do his first FIREBALL SPIN.

We all watched as Rojo got faster and faster and FASTER and then he leapt into the air and spun round

SUPER FAST.

That's when I saw the smoke. I couldn't believe it! Rojo's new costume had a built-in SMOKE MACHINE to make him look even MORE like a real fireball.

Everyone cheered.

But then someone yelled, "Rojo's on FIRE!"

Everyone RAN on to the ice. Clem got to Rojo first and she stamped ALL OVER him until the smoking stopped.

Rojo looked a bit shocked. But then he smiled and said, "I cannot believe that I am now so good at spinning that I have set my new costume on FIRE!"

"Um, I don't think that's EXACTLY what happened," said Clem.

Before Clem could say any more, Jasmine and Gerard pushed in.

"Oh, ROJO!" wailed Jasmine. "You poor LAMB CHOP! You must see a vet AT

ONCE!"

Rojo said he was fine but before he could even finish his sentence Gerard picked him up and skated away really fast.

"Now, I don't want ANY of you little blossoms to worry about dear, sweet Rojo," Jasmine said. "I've called the BEST VET money can buy and she's going to bandage up all those nasty-looking burns and I'm SURE that in a few weeks Rojo will be as good as new!"

EVERYONE started clapping and thanking Jasmine for phoning the vet and getting Rojo help so quickly.

But not Clem. Clem was doing that low growly thing she does sometimes when she's

SUPER ANNOYED.

"First it's DISAPPEARING ICE
SKATES and now A FIRE, all in one day,"
said Jasmine. "I'm starting to think this ice
rink might be HAUNTED."

That's when Clem said, "Follow me,
Pugly. This is SERIOUS."

Once we were in the dressing room, Clem locked the door and began checking in all the cupboards AND the drawers AND behind the sofa.

At first I thought she was checking for GHOSTS but then Clem said we needed to make sure NO ONE ELSE was in the room because she had something SUPER SERIOUS to tell me.

"She's lying," said Clem.

"Who's lying?" I asked.

Clem rolled her eyes at me.

"JASMINE!" she hissed. "There was NO NEED to call a vet! Rojo wasn't hurt at ALL. He didn't even have one tiny burn. When I got to him there was a tiny flame at the end of one of the ribbons on his costume, but I stamped it out before it got anywhere NEAR his body!"

I said that Jasmine was obviously just trying to be nice and that she wanted to make sure Rojo was OK. Then I asked Clem if she thought Jasmine might be right about the haunted ice rink because I am

<u>TOTALLY</u>

<u>SCARED</u>

OF GHOSTS.

Clem looked over both of her shoulders to make sure no one was listening.

"There's NO GHOST, Pugly. It was SABOTAGE!" she hissed. "Jasmine set FIRE to Rojo's costume on PURPOSE. She wants him OUT of the competition."

I was SHOCKED. Then she came so close to my face I could smell her TUNA BREATH. "Guess what Rojo told me before he started skating? He said his NEW SKATING OUTFIT was a GIFT from JASMINE and GERARD!"

Chapter 7

I couldn't BELIEVE it. Jasmine and Gerard had SABOTAGED Rojo's performance.

"Why would they DO that, Clem?" I asked.

Clem narrowed her eyes and stared at me. "Because they want to WIN, that's why. Rojo was doing too well. They didn't like that. So they got rid of him. They're

CHEATERS, Pugly!"

"We need to tell the judges RIGHT
AWAY!" I said, rushing past Clem to the
door.

Clem POUNCED and knocked me to the
floor. "We can't tell ANYONE," she hissed.
"Do you hear me?"

I nodded that I did because Clem had me
PINNED to the ground.

"The judges won't believe us because
they LOVE Jasmine and Gerard too much.
They'll think we're LYING."

"But … but … we're
NOT lying!"
I said.

"THEY are the ones who are LYING.
They're pretending to be nice but really
they are PURE EVIL! It's not FAIR."

Clem's tail went COMPLETEY
STRAIGHT all of a sudden.

"TINY," she whispered.

I looked around but I couldn't
see Tiny anywhere.

"I've just realised something," Clem whispered. "It WASN'T an accident. It was THEM. They STOLE Tiny's lucky ice skates. They KNEW she wouldn't skate without them!"

I was SHOCKED. Poor Tiny.

Those evil greyhounds had to be STOPPED!

"We need to catch Jasmine and Gerard in the

ACT OF SABOTAGE,"

said Clem. "We can take a photo as EVIDENCE and then the judges will HAVE to believe us."

"But how are we going to catch them?" I asked.

Clem narrowed her eyes again, which meant she was thinking HARD.

56

Chapter 8

I sat nervously at the side of the rink with Clem as Hugo the sausage dog began his routine.

I started to relax as I watched. I LOVE watching Hugo skate because he is SUPER FUNNY and he wears goggles for no particular reason which is HILARIOUS! And he's got this REALLY LONG stripy scarf that flaps around when he skates, and when he does a belly slide he wraps it around his WHOLE SAUSAGE-DOGGY BODY!

Every time Hugo did a BELLY SLIDE across the ice the crowd CHEERED and everyone giggled, even Clem.

Everything was going well, and I'd completely forgotten about the Jasmine and Gerard sabotage thing, until Hugo did his BELLY SLIDE FINALE.

JUST as Hugo began to slide across the ice the whole room went PITCH BLACK.

"CLEM!" I cried. "What's HAPPENING?"

There was a horrible CRASHING SOUND.

Then all of a sudden the lights flickered and went back on and EVERYONE gasped because Hugo had crashed RIGHT THROUGH the side of the rink … and he was STUCK!

"Hugo!" I cried. I jumped over the barrier and rushed to help him.

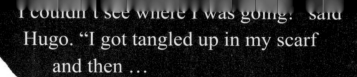

I couldn't see where I was going!" said Hugo. "I got tangled up in my scarf and then …

SMACK!"

It was really weird seeing Hugo stuck in the wall like that because sausage dogs are so LONG that he sort of looked like TWO dogs; one with only legs and a head sticking out one side of the wall and another with just legs and a tail sticking out the other side.

"Well, don't just stare, Pugly," said Clem. "Help me get him OUT!"

So me and Clem helped squeeze Hugo through the wall until he was just one dog again.

"Just as well I was wearing THESE!" said Hugo as he took off his goggles. "What HAPPENED?"

The judges said that there must have been a POWER CUT and that they were sorry about his accident and that he could do his routine for Round Two again.

But Hugo said that he was a bit dizzy and

that his NOSE was hurting from crashing
into the wall and that he didn't want to do
the competition any more.

"It's the GHOST!"

cried Jasmine.

"It's STRUCK AGAIN!"

Everyone began whispering about the ghost and looking worriedly around the ice rink.

"Pugly," said Jasmine, with a tear in her eye. "We must STICK TOGETHER and not let this ICE GHOST scare us. Even though ghosts are PRETTY SCARY, aren't they, Pugly?"

I gulped because she was right – ghosts ARE pretty scary. Jasmine patted my head and said that I needed to be brave, even though the ghost was probably after ME, too!

Chapter 9

The judges said there would be a break in the competition for lunch. I changed out of my sparkly leotard in case I got my sandwich on it while Hugo was taken away on a stretcher.

"Don't panic, Pugly," said Clem. I WAS panicking. "It wasn't a GHOST. Jasmine switched the lights off so that Hugo would crash! We have to stop her NOW!"

So I told Clem that Jasmine couldn't have switched off the lights because she'd been standing at the side of the ice rink when it happened. And that's when we both realised GERARD must do all the SABOTAGING instead!

"THAT'S why HE'S so quiet all the time," said Clem.

"He's like a SPY or a SECRET AGENT.

NO ONE NOTICES HIM because they're too busy listening to Jasmine!"

Clem was RIGHT.

"All we have to do is follow Gerard," I said. "He'll lead us right to their next EVIL SABOTAGE!"

Clem agreed. "Right, let's get ready!" she said.

We arrived at my dressing room just as a
WHITE SHEET ran out of the door and
down the corridor.

I GASPED because I thought it was a

REAL GHOST!

ᘓᘓᘓᘓᘓᘓᘓ

But then I noticed that the ghost had
GREYHOUND
FEET!

We RACED into the dressing room to see if everything was OK.

It definitely WASN'T.

My dressing room was COMPLETELY TRASHED!

And my glittery costume was

IN SHREDS!

I was FURIOUS but not as furious as CLEM was! She marched into Jasmine's dressing room and waved the leotard under her nose. "YOU DID THIS!" she hissed.

"How DARE you!" said Jasmine. "I would NEVER destroy such a beautiful leotard! Anyway, I was with the judges this WHOLE TIME. So how could I have done it? Hmmm?"

And then she smiled a REALLY CREEPY smile at me and left.

Chapter 10

"I think it might be time for me to just quit the competition," I said to Clem. "I mean, I'm OBVIOUSLY not going to win ANYWAY and now I don't have anything to wear."

Clem walked up to me REALLY SLOWLY and turned me around to face the mirror.

"LOOK at yourself, Pugly," she said, in a very serious voice.

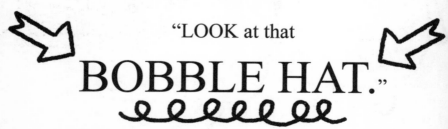

"LOOK at that

BOBBLE HAT."

I looked at myself in the mirror.

"That's not the hat of a quitter!" she said.
"You're a

PUG.

ℓℓℓℓℓℓℓℓ

And PUGS don't quit because of
BIG BULLY GREYHOUNDS!"

∿∿∿∿∿∿∿∿∿

Her voice was getting louder and louder.
"We haven't been able to prove that
Jasmine and Gerard are CHEATING but
there IS something that we CAN do to
teach those greedy greyhounds a lesson."

I spun round and looked at her. "What?
What can we do?!"

"We can WIN!" said Clem.

"But CLEEEM," I said. "I STILL don't
know what MY special thing is!"

"I do," said Clem quietly. And then she
disappeared into the wardrobe.

When she came back out I COULDN'T
BELIEVE IT. She was wearing a
LEOTARD and a little CAT SKIRT. And
she had on sparkly red ICE SKATES!
  "I thought maybe I could be your
SPECIAL THING," said Clem, shyly.
"We'd be the first dog and cat ice-skating
pair to ever
enter *Pets
on Ice*. And
I know that
for a fact
because I
checked."

I was MEGA CONFUSED because I had NO IDEA that Clem wanted to be my SKATING PARTNER.

"Clem, why didn't you TELL ME that you wanted to skate?" I asked.

Clem inspected her paws carefully, which is what she does if she's feeling a little bit unsure.

"You didn't ask me," she said in a tiny voice.

I felt TERRIBLE when Clem said that because I hadn't realised at ALL that Clem wanted to be my skating partner.

"I'm so sorry, Clem," I said. "I didn't realise you liked ice skating so much."

"I LOVE ICE SKATING!" she said. "You get to go SUPER FAST and do TWIRLS and SLIDES and LEAPS and WHY DO YOU THINK I GAVE YOU THOSE ICE SKATES!"

Clem stopped talking and held out
something sparkly and red.

It was a

NEW
PUGTASTIC
LEOTARD!

I gasped.

"And I've made up our very own ROUTINE. It's a NEW thing. No one else does it. But I don't know if you'll like it."

It was weird seeing Clem being nervous because Clem is NEVER nervous. I knew that must mean that Clem REALLY wanted to be my ice-skating partner and that it was really important to her.

"Will you show me?" I asked.

Clem passed me a pad of paper. She'd made LOADS of sketches of me and her on the ice doing LOADS of different things.

"Do you like it?" asked Clem eagerly.

"No," I said, looking right at Clem. "I don't like it… I LOVE IT! Let's go BEAT those CHEATING GREYHOUNDS!"

Chapter 11

On our way to the rink we banged

RIGHT into GERARD.

"Oh, sorry," he said, quietly.

I realised that this was the first time I'd heard Gerard SPEAK.

"Um, it's OK," I said, picking up the bottle of water Gerard had dropped on the ground and handing it to him.

"Thanks," he mumbled, and put it in his training bag.

Clem looked at me like I was MAD for helping Gerard, but there was something about him that made me feel bad for him.

"Gerard, are you OK?" I asked.

Gerard looked up at me with worried eyes, but he didn't say anything.

I looked at Clem. She was STARING at something in Gerard's bag.

Gerard caught Clem staring and tried to leave. But before he could move

ONE GREYHOUND
MUSCLE

Clem pulled something out of his bag with her claw.

It was a WHITE SHEET with two EYE-HOLES cut in it!

Clem turned to me with a HUGE smile on her face and then she said,

"EVIDENCE!"

But then Gerard BURST OUT CRYING.

"PLEASE don't tell the judges," he whimpered. "PLEASE!"

Clem narrowed her eyes at him. "Why SHOULDN'T we?" she hissed. "You SABOTAGED all the other contestants' acts just so YOU EVIL GREYHOUNDS could win *Pets on Ice*!"

"It's JASMINE!

She made me do it!" bawled Gerard. "She's OBSESSED with winning. If I don't do what she wants she SCREAMS at me just because she's the OLDER TWIN by ONE MINUTE."

I stared at Clem. I wasn't sure what we should do.

"Are you scared of Jasmine?" I said.

Gerard nodded.

"I don't even LIKE ice skating," he sobbed. "I want to be a footballer."

I put my hand on Gerard's shoulder.

"Gerard, you have to stand up to her. And you have to tell the judges that it was you who caused the accidents, OK?"

"I can't!" said Gerard, looking panicked. "I'm so sorry, Pugly. But I'm just too SCARED of the SCREAMING. But I

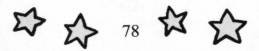

PROMISE not to do anything else to help
Jasmine.

I PROMISE!"

Then Gerard ran off down the corridor.

I turned to Clem. She still had the Ghost Sheet in her paw.

"What now?" I asked her. "Should we take the sheet to the judges and tell them what's been going on?"

But Clem said that she wasn't sure because Gerard had OBVIOUSLY been forced to do the SABOTAGING by Jasmine.

"Jasmine will probably just LIE and tell the judges it was all Gerard's fault," said Clem. "And then they'll only punish Gerard, and Jasmine will get away with it."

Clem hid the sheet in my training bag before anyone could see.

"Let's just stick to our original plan," said Clem. "Let's go out there and BEAT Jasmine and WIN *Pets on Ice* and THAT will show her!"

Chapter 12

The crowd went WILD when Jasmine and Gerard skated on to the ice for the final round. They were SCREAMING Jasmine's name and throwing RED ROSES at her.

Clem looked at me and
I knew EXACTLY what
she was thinking because I was
thinking the same thing. Jasmine's
fans had NO IDEA how EVIL and
SABOTAGE-Y she REALLY was.

Clem and I watched
nervously from the side
as Jasmine and Gerard began
skating. The crowd cheered every
time Jasmine TWIRLED and Gerard
LEAPT.

They were good. REALLY good.

  83

I looked at Clem. She was up on the barrier watching closely. She had her little matching leotard on and she'd covered herself in glitter, just like me.

I REALLY wanted to win. And I didn't even want to win for ME any more. I wanted to win for Clem.

I pulled Clem's sketches out of my training bag and studied the pictures carefully. I HAD to get this right. I didn't want to let Clem down.

"Pugly … look at this," said Clem. "I think there's something wrong."

I looked up and saw Jasmine twirling Gerard around and around. But Gerard wasn't smiling. And Gerard USUALLY smiles ALL THE TIME when they are skating.

I watched as Jasmine let Gerard's hands go so he could do his TRIPLE

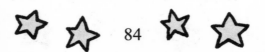

84

BACKWARDS FLIP.

But Gerard didn't do his TRIPLE flip. He just did ONE flip and then landed on his

BOTTOM!

The crowd

GASPED!

Gerard got up and rubbed his bottom. "I'm sorry," he said. "I've hurt my bottom. I can't go on."

I looked at Jasmine. Her face was RED with ANGER.

The judges discussed Jasmine and Gerard's score for a while before eventually holding up a five.

Jasmine RUSHED off the ice when she saw the score. Gerard looked over at us and gave us a tiny smile just as Jasmine pulled him off the rink behind her.

I turned and looked at Clem. Her mouth was hanging wide open.

"You don't think Gerard did that on PURPOSE do you?"

But Clem didn't get a chance to answer me because that's when the announcer said, "AND NOW IT'S TIME FOR THE LAST ROUTINE. It's PUGL— Um… Wait. I see there's been a LAST MINUTE change here. Pugly is now part of a PAIR," said the judge.

The crowd GASPED.

"PLEASE
WELCOME
ON TO THE ICE …

PUGLY AND

CLEM!"

The crowd cheered as me and Clem skated on to the ice.

But when the judges saw Clem they looked SHOCKED. And so did JASMINE!

"Hold on a MINUTE!" yelled Jasmine, skating over to the judges. "CATS aren't allowed in this competition! It's for DOGS!"

Jasmine looked TOTALLY
flustered. Her hair had fallen down and
she looked a bit sweaty.

I looked at Clem. She was looking down
at her paws.

"EXCUSE me," I said to Jasmine. "But
this competition is called *PETS on Ice*,
not *DOGS on Ice*. It doesn't MATTER if
you're a CAT or a DOG or a GUINEA PIG.
ANY pet can take part!"

Big Sal the guinea pig and all his friends

cheered from the back of the crowd
when I said that.

"Pugly's RIGHT," said the judges. "This
competition isn't just for dogs. CATS are
welcome. And so are all other pets, for that
matter."

The crowd cheered and Jasmine gave us a
LOOK and stormed off the ice.

"Good luck, Clem," I said as we waited
to start.

Clem reached up and whispered in my ear, "Thanks. You too. Now… When the lights go down DON'T PANIC, OK? It's a surprise!"

I had

NO IDEA

what Clem was up to.
But I was

EXCITED!

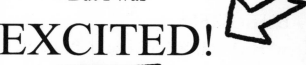

Chapter 13

As soon as Clem and I started skating around the ice, paw in paw, I realised that I was having the BEST FUN EVER!

It wasn't even difficult because Clem knew EXACTLY what she was doing and she floated around me like an ICY BUTTERFLY.

"Hey, Pugly," she said. "LOOK!" And then she did a TRIPLE BACKWARDS somersault JUST like Gerard and Jasmine did!

The crowd CHEERED and Clem winked at me.

"I've been watching all of the contestants REALLY closely," she said, grinning. "I've learnt a thing or two!"

She definitely HAD. She was AWESOME! And it wasn't long before everyone was chanting our names and clapping along!

Clem and I skated backwards together, waving to the crowd, all the way around the rink, TWICE! Clem put that in our routine because she knew skating backwards was my FAVOURITE.

Then Clem turned to me and said, "It's time for our FINALE. Are you ready?"

I nodded that I was even though I had NO IDEA what was about to happen.

All of a sudden the music got really LOUD and FAST and the lights went down a bit and the crowd went quiet. They were EXCITED. And so was I!

Clem grabbed my paw
and we SPED around the rink
at SUPER FAST SPEED with a
SPOTLIGHT following us the

ENTIRE TIME!

Then the music changed again and a giant DISCO BALL came down from the roof and made everything SPARKLY and me and Clem held hands and spun around and around laughing the WHOLE TIME!

The crowd went WILD!

"CLEM!" I cried. "How did you DO all of this?"

Clem flipped around and began skating backwards and pointed up to a little glass booth near the roof that I'd never seen before. "Wave to Tim!" she said. "Tim controls the music and the lights and all the tech stuff. I noticed him working so I went up and introduced myself."

I waved at Tim and the lights flashed BRIGHT PINK back at me and the crowd gasped with delight. "OK, this is IT," said Clem, excitedly. "I hope it WORKS!"

Clem jumped on to my shoulders and told

96

me to skate around the rink backwards as
SOON as the lights went down.

Then the lights went down. The crowd
began to whisper.

"GO!" said Clem.

I had no idea what Clem was doing on my shoulders as I skated but then I heard the crowd GASP and applaud LOADS.

I looked up at Clem.

She was waving her paws at the audience.

That's when I noticed that she had GLOW-IN-THE-DARK CLAWS!

"CLEM!" I cried. "That's SO COOL! I love it!"

"Really?" said Clem. "WELL. If you liked that you'll LOVE this!"

Clem started WHIZZING her paws around at LIGHTNING SPEED, leaving trails of COLOUR in the air as we FLEW along the ice.

That's when I noticed Clem was WRITING something in the air, over and over again, and EVERYONE was on their feet taking pictures and whistling and cheering.

Clem was writing *PUGLY ON ICE*!

"You guys ROCK!" screamed voices
from the side of the rink.

Clem and I looked over and saw that Tiny, Hugo and Rojo were all back and watching us from the side!

"You are THE BEST!" yelled Rojo.

Even the JUDGES were on their feet!

It was AMAZING!

When the lights came back on Clem and I stood paw in paw as we waited for the judges to hold up our score.

Jasmine and Gerard had got a five so we had to beat that.

Clem's paw felt SWEATY in mine, but I didn't mind because I was nervous TOO.

"We the judges have NEVER seen ANYTHING like what we have seen tonight," said the Head Judge. "Not only are Pugly and Clem the first ever dog and cat ice-skating pair … they are now the first ever dog and cat *Pets on Ice* CHAMPIONS! TEN OUT OF TEN!"

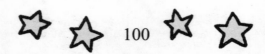

The crowd exploded with applause and absolutely COVERED US in flowers and confetti and someone even threw their HAT at me (which was awesome because it was a VERY nice hat).

"CLEM!" I screamed.

"WE WON!"

Clem was grinning from ear to ear.

But there was ONE person who was NOT happy.

"GET OUT OF MY WAY!" shouted Jasmine as she barged past all the other contestants who had skated on to the ice to congratulate us.

"LOOK!" she said as she dropped something on the judges' table.

It was my training bag. The Ghost Sheet that Clem had put in there was hanging out, and Tiny's lucky skates were there too.

"What do you call THESE?" said Jasmine, yanking the skates out and holding them up for the judges to see.

The judges looked at Tiny's skates, and then at me, with concerned faces.

"I DIDN'T TAKE THEM!" I cried.

"Well, they were found in YOUR bag," said Jasmine.

Clem squeezed my paw and gave me a LOOK. She wanted me to tell the judges about Gerard. But I didn't want to get Gerard into trouble. I felt bad for him.

"I didn't take them, I PROMISE!" I said, but the judges just shook their heads at me.

"This is grounds for immediate DISQUALIFICATION," said the Head Judge.

Clem GASPED. She was panicking. And so was I! We were about to be DISQUALIFIED!

"It was ME!" shouted Gerard. He skated up to the judges. "I took the skates and sabotaged the competition. But SHE forced me," he said, pointing to Jasmine. "She BULLIES me and I've had ENOUGH."

"So you DID fall on purpose!" said Clem.

Gerard nodded. "Tiny, Rojo, Hugo … I cannot apologise enough for what I did to you. Please forgive me."

Jasmine's face went ALL sorts of colours. She was FURIOUS.

Her hair looked WILD and her mascara was running down her sweaty, angry face.

"THAT'S IT!" screamed Jasmine. "I've had enough of YOU," she said, pointing to Gerard. "And I've had enough of you silly JUDGES.

"In fact, I've had ENOUGH of ALL OF YOU!" she said, pointing to the crowd. "I am AMAZING and I should win

EVERYTHING! None of you even know the FIRST THING about ice skating. I am an expert! I am the best! I AM JASMINE!" she screamed.

The crowd fell absolutely silent for a second. And then they began booing.

A LOT!

"You can't boo ME!" shrieked Jasmine.

"Miss Jasmine, you are officially disqualified from *Pets on Ice* for LIFE! Now please LEAVE," said the Head Judge.

Jasmine went BERSERK when two security guards escorted her out of the rink. But I completely IGNORED her because I'd had QUITE enough of that spoiled greyhound.

That's when Clem whispered something to the judges that made them smile.

"We are pleased to announce that Clem and Pugly will be sharing their prize – a lifetime's supply of TREATS – with their friends Rojo, Hugo and Tiny! Well done EVERYONE!"

"Hey, Pugly," said Clem. "Give me some paw!"

And I giggled and high-fived her.

Bonus Chapter!

Dear Pugly & Clem,

I want to invite you both to my first football match next week. I am LOVING football!

Guess what?

Jasmine is teaching ice skating to PUPPIES now and they NEVER do what she says… It's HILARIOUS to watch!

Love Gerard

x x x